OVER ALL THE EARTH

A TALE OF THE CHANTS

OVER ALL THE EARTH

A TALE OF THE CHANTS

ALEXANDRA ROWLAND

ISBN: 978-1-957461-01-4

www.alexandrarowland.net

CONTENTS

OVER ALL THE EARTH

JUST AS SUMMER WAS turning golden and easing into autumn, a stranger came to the village—that event alone was enough for Eisl's curiosity to be stirred for a number of reasons, and all of them had to do with the bridge.

Eisl's village was way up in the mountains, tucked on a broad ledge between craggy cliffs on one side and the great ravine on the other side. The ledge, which the villagers just called the Ledge, bore little more than a band of forest and a few tiny farms, mostly kitchen gardens—the soil was thin and rocky, and the peaks and crags soaring high above blocked out too much light. Goatherding and mining were the primary occupations

—Eisl had tried both, and hated both, and begrudgingly decided he hated the goats slightly less than the mines.

He would have left if he could. He could have been a carter and taken the ore and cheese down to the market town; that wouldn't have been so bad. Even if he'd been tasked with taking the goats down to the butcher, that wouldn't have been so bad.

But he could not leave, and that too was because of the bridge.

It was a bridge of ropes and vines and planks, and it was the only way to get in or out of the village without climbing down the face of the ravine and following the river... Eisl had heard that there were two waterfalls that way, which also would have to be scaled if one wished to take that path. Eisl was afraid of heights. Eisl had never left his village on his own two feet, though he longed to see the market again—he had one faint memory of it from childhood—toddlerhood, really.

It had been so *huge* and so *bright* and so colorful, without all the deep green trees and almost perpetual misty cloud-haze and the looming peaks above to choke out the sky and sun. The ever-present distant roar of the river at the bottom of the ravine had been absent too—that was the most astounding thing, even in memory. Even with the chatter and human bustle of the market, it had seemed so astonishingly *silent.*

But regardless of how alluring the memory of the market town was, how wistfully Eisl thought of occupying himself with some industry besides mining or goatherding, he just could not bring himself to cross the bridge, nor to climb down the side of the ravine wall either.

The bridge was *so* terrifying, in fact, that he was by turns fascinated with and infuriated by people who did cross it, including the rare stranger who trekked up from the market town—but they were never *really* strangers. They always knew someone in the village or had business there with the mine. They were strangers in that it was profoundly strange to see someone that Eisl did not know personally and that he had not seen every single day since he'd been born.

This stranger, though. This was a *new* stranger—a properly strange stranger.

Eisl had herded the goats up the slope towards the grazing meadow, an area of the Ledge that had been cleared for pastures and a few fields, as it was the only place on the ledge that got sun for more than two or three hours a day. The bridge was a distant thread across the mist-choked ravine. Generally he avoided looking at it, but as he was sitting there with the goats, something caught his eye.

He saw the stranger on the bridge.

He knew immediately that it was a stranger, even so far away. They had stopped in the middle of the bridge, facing up the ravine. Eisl couldn't tell what they were doing, but it stopped his heart dead in his chest even to imagine lingering in the middle of the bridge like that.

There was... *something* in the ravine, it was said. A god, perhaps, or a spirit. Something or *someone* that had soaked into the land. Twice a year, at the spring and autumn equinoxes, the villagers made offerings to the god of the ravine—sweet honey cakes, and goat cheese, and bits of ore from the mine. Sometimes pretty things bought in the market town, too, because they thought that might be extra lucky. Eisl had not made offerings in... years and years. He avoided the bridge and the edge of the ravine whenever possible—even thirty feet from the edge was far too close for comfort.

The stranger stood there for nearly ten minutes—by which point, someone from the village passing nearby had noticed and was standing at the head of the bridge and gesturing emphatically for the stranger to finish crossing.

At length, they did, and they and the villager were hidden by the pines.

I N THE EVENING, EISL brought the goats down from the pasture—safer than leaving them on the slope, where there could be wolves or landslides or sudden gales or any manner of disaster—and went looking for the stranger. It was not yet sunset, and the sky above was still light enough to distinguish it from the mountain peaks, but the shadows were as thick as twilight down on the Ledge.

"Someone came today?" he said to the first person he came across—Lisen, one of his cousins, who would be on her way home from the smithy for dinner—even as she opened her mouth to speak.

"Yes!" she said, breathlessly excited. "I was just about to tell you! How did you know? Did you see him crossing from the pasture? You must have—oh, Eisl, everyone's talking about him! He's a *storyteller*."

"Where is he?"

"At Pollot's," she said, and before the last syllable was out of her mouth, Eisl was rushing past her to what passed for the village's alehouse.

It was full of grubby miners and warm golden light—the warmest place on the whole ledge, Eisl had always thought. Usually it was full of chatter and laughter and life—or grim, bleak silence, if there had been some accident down in the mine—but tonight the silence was rich and thick with some kind of energy that made the hair stand up on the back of Eisl's neck and all down his arms, that made the breath catch in his chest before he was even two steps inside.

Silence, yes, but razor-sharp, heavy, hungry. A few pairs of eyes flicked to him as he came in the door; Eisl got a few nods or smiles before all eyes turned back to... the stranger.

He was a young man, a couple of years younger than Eisl. He had pale skin like the southern lowlanders, golden hair that was long enough to fall into his face, and eyes of the most extraordinary rich blue—bluer than the center of the sky on a clear day. As blue as twilight. He was tallish, but not extraordinarily so; he was pleasant enough to look at, but not extraordinarily handsome. He looked like any reasonably comely young man—there were a few who brought up supplies from the town, and the stranger could have been one of them. (*They* rarely crossed the bridge. They left that to the villagers.)

But the stranger with the twilight-blue eyes had a *something* about him that made it impossible to look away from him. It wasn't like heat radiating off a fire, or light from the sun, or the roar of the river. It was a still thing, a quiet thing, like the force that made ripples die down out of the surface of the water.

This stranger had that force, whatever it was, and it was keeping any small ripples from shivering through the crowd.

Magic? Maybe that's what it was.

The stranger had a cup of Pollot's beer in front of him, cupped between his hands. There was a plate of bread and cheese beside him, and a half-empty bowl—likely Pollot's goat stew.

The stranger was speaking. He was telling some story about something that had happened in the lowlands. The road down the mountain was arduous and slow; no one left unless they had business in town, so news of the wide world was rare and interesting.

"—but they fixed the dike and kept the water back, so all was well. Let's see, what else? Oh, I heard from one of my colleagues that the sultan of Araşt gave birth to a daughter. That would have been... a little more than a year ago, I believe?"

"What's a sultan?" someone whispered.

"Oh, a monarch. A queen, in this case," said the stranger.

"Where's Araşt?" someone else asked in a louder, gruffer voice.

The stranger traced a few lines on the table, broke off pieces of bread and cheese for markers, and explained— he showed them where they were, on the eastern side of the Wall of the World (which was apparently what people called the mountains here—Eisl had never heard this; they were only *the mountains* to him, because why distinguish these ones from any others? They were too tall and uniform to distinguish individual masses anyway, and the smaller crags weren't worth naming). He showed them, even farther east by hundreds and hundreds of miles, the coastline—the Amethyst Sea, he said, and the Sea of Storms.

"On the other side of the Wall," the stranger said, "if you were able to climb over the mountains and go west from here, you'd find an enormous desert."

"What's a desert?" Eisl heard himself asking. The stranger looked up and met his eyes—he blinked and smiled. Oh, he had a nice smile. Eisl was sure, suddenly, that the stranger was a very, very kind person. It was in the way he smiled so gently, like he was pleased to be asked and not at all thinking of teasing Eisl for his ignorance—though if he'd tried to tease, it would have been an insult to the whole room. No one else knew what a desert was either. Eisl himself barely knew what an *ocean* was—like a pond, but a lot bigger. It was where the river went, eventually. He knew that much.

"When you look out from the slope of the mountains here," said the stranger, "the world rolls out before you, green hills and forests and fields as far as the eye can see. Right?" Eisl nodded; others in the room nodded too, caught in that pulling, stilling-ripples force the stranger had. "Imagine that the rolling hills were as golden as a wheat field, but made of sand and gravel and rock. Imagine that it was as hot as sitting next to a fire on a summer day. Imagine that it was dry as a jerky-hut. It never rains in the desert, so growing things are rare and tough and scraggly, like the plants that grow high, high up on the mountain."

"The plants only goats can eat," Eisl said, nodding in understanding.

The stranger paused and seemed to look at him a second time. A flicker of something passed across his face; a moment of wry amusement, though it was gone again instantly. Then he *did* give Eisl another look, a third one, this one more deliberate, dragging his eyes down Eisl's body and back up to his face as a light of interest kindled in his twilight-eyes. "Yes," he said, as if answering some inside-joke he had with himself. "That sort of plant. Are you yourself a goatherd, then?"

Eisl wished he could say no. He wished—oh, he wished to be *anything* but a goatherd. "Yes," he said. *For now,* he wanted to add, but that would only make everyone in the room laugh.

The stranger smiled to himself and lowered his eyes. "The desert, then. Beyond that is grasslands, and if you keep heading straight west, you pass through the jungle —that's like a forest, but hot and wet and so full of life that you would not believe such a thing was possible. If you keep going west, when you exit the jungle you will find another ocean—the Sea of Serpents. Follow the coastline north and eventually you will come to Araşt." Another one of those wry, private-joke smiles as he said,

"If you hit the footlands of the Mountains of Mirhalaş, you've gone too far." Several of the others in the room looked at each other in confusion, but Eisl laughed—though he didn't know why he was laughing or what the joke was.

The stranger looked up again and smiled at him.

T HE STRANGER TRIED TO tell them legends, but always someone would interrupt to ask what such-and-such thing was, or what the animal the stranger had mentioned looked like, and so on. He seemed to realize this with an impressive swiftness, concluding that they were hungry for stories of the *world,* that every word he told them about the lands he'd seen and the peoples of it seemed to stretch out the horizons farther, and farther, and then farther still... until the world grew bigger and more vast than they had ever imagined, yet still small enough to fit inside their heads. At least, that was how it felt for Eisl.

Finally, when it was properly night-time and getting a bit late, the stranger remembered his beer and drank half of it in a gulp. The alehouse was packed with all of Eisl's kith and kin—there were even more of them now than there had been when Eisl had arrived; half the village had tried to cram inside. With an endearingly shy look at all of them, the stranger said, "I'd be happy to tell you more stories tomorrow, but it was rather a hard path up the mountain—they didn't tell me down in the village how steep it was!"

"The town, you mean?" Eisl said; he'd drifted up slowly, pulled helplessly forward to the table as the stranger spoke, and then someone had given him their chair.

"Riverhead Village, they said it was called," said the stranger thoughtfully. "The one right at the bottom of the path."

"Yes—we call that 'the town'. I guess because it's bigger than us." Riverhead Village, Eisl mused to himself. He'd never heard that name before. "What do they call us?"

"The folks up on the ledge," said the stranger with a laugh.

"That's right enough, I guess," Eisl said, gesturing to Pollot for a cup of beer.

"And you? What do you call yourselves?"

"Just the folks on the ledge, I suppose," he sighed.

T HE STRANGER WAS... ENCHANTING, in the sense that Eisl felt he had been ensnared by magic. Attractive, in the sense of some mysterious force pulling Eisl towards him.

Attractive in the sense of handsome, too, but Eisl had never flirted with *anyone* before. The boys in his village liked the girls in his village, and that was that. Eisl had felt frustration and longing through all his youth and hadn't even known that boys *could* like boys until one of the people who brought supplies up to the ledge arrived just as a storm was looming over the mountains—he'd had to cross the bridge and stay the night at Pollot's place, and Eisl had overheard him talking to someone about how worried his husband was going to be. A great crashing wave of *ohhh!* had slammed into him, and many things in the world suddenly made a lot more sense.

The stranger seemed to like boys too—he kept giving Eisl these... these *looks*, warm and appreciative and intriguing, and somehow Eisl knew exactly what they meant. He was thrilled, terrified, exhilarated, *starving*. He wondered if this stranger might... touch him, or kiss him, or... or lie down with him in the hayloft and be close to him.

"Would you like to go for a walk?" Eisl asked awkwardly, because that's what the boys and girls of the village often asked each other when they wanted to be alone.

"Love to," the stranger said in a low voice, looking right into Eisl's eyes.

Eisl lost his courage as soon as they stepped out of Pollot's, but the stranger seemed to know what he was doing—he took Eisl's hand, and they strolled off into the dark. "Where shall we walk to?" the stranger asked lightly. "It gets a little chilly at night in these mountains."

Eisl gulped. "We could... sit in my uncle's hayloft?"

"That sounds cozy." A moment later, he squeezed Eisl's hand and said, "Your pulse is like a frightened rabbit's."

"I'm fine," Eisl said. "I'm fine."

"Shy?" the stranger whispered, squeezing his hand again and bumping their shoulders together.

That was easier than admitting he'd never done anything like this before. Eisl nodded.

"We can just sit and talk if you want," the stranger said, smiling at him.

Eisl's heart stopped for one panicked moment; he shook his head violently. "No—no, I—" He'd never met a boy who looked at him like that; what if he never met a second one?

The stranger's smile widened, almost fond. He bit his lip, glanced around, and then caught Eisl around the waist and backed him against a tree. "How about now? Still shy?" he asked—his eyes were so terribly blue, so terribly warm and inviting. Eisl was trembling from head to toe, but diving in to kiss the stranger was... irresistible. As irresistible as an avalanche.

H E WAS LAUGHING BY the time he dragged the stranger into the barn and up the ladder into the hayloft—both of them were laughing. Eisl grabbed at him, already greedy for another kiss, another press of someone's heat and weight against him. He was still shaking. It was less with terror now, just singing want and the heady thrill.

The stranger let Eisl bowl him over into the hay, giggling. "What's the rush?"

"I don't know," Eisl said breathlessly, crushing his mouth against the stranger's. "You're so—I just—I've never seen someone so—" He shuddered all over with desire and buried his face against the stranger's neck. He smelled of the pines and fresh air and warm young man, but Eisl imagined that underneath all of that he could smell all the intriguing scents of strange and far-off places, richer and more wonderful than he had ever imagined.

The stranger hummed and tipped his head aside, baring his neck; Eisl heard himself making a soft noise of desire and opened his mouth to taste the stranger's skin. "What's your name?" he murmured, feeling half-delirious. "I didn't ask—sorry—I should have asked—"

The stranger laughed, catching on a gasp as Eisl's teeth scraped across his skin. "That's a complicated question—which one do you want?"

"What's that mean?" Eisl said, muffled against the stranger's skin.

"I have—oh—options for you to choose from, you can have--" He caught on another breathless laugh and slid his hands into Eisl's hair, "—you can have the name that's means me, or the name that means what I am."

Eisl couldn't think, didn't want to think, didn't want anything but... everything. "Both, both, all of it," he said —it was like being drunk. He had never felt more alive, never.

"Ylfing," gasped the stranger as Eisl mouthed greedily at his neck so he'd make that *oh* noise again. "Or Chant."

Something in Eisl trembled again, another want, a different kind—one that was thinner, reedier, crisper than the all-consuming desire to touch and be touched, to want and be wanted. "Ylfing," he whispered against the stranger's skin. "Chant."

"Kiss me again," said Ylfing. So he did.

A FTERWARDS, THEY LAY IN the prickly hay and breathed together in the dark.

"Why do you have two names?" Eisl asked—he'd caught his breath, but he was still pleasantly glowing with warmth and relaxation.

"I told you—one is who I am, and one is what I do. Chant is a... a title, I suppose you could say. A label. Like farmer, or cooper, or blacksmith."

"What is it? What does a Chant do?"

"What you saw me doing earlier in the tavern," Ylfing said, laughing a little. Eisl heard him shift in the hay, turning towards him. "A Chant wanders from place to place and tells stories and... looks for new ones."

"Why?"

There was a long pause. A huff of breath—Eisl couldn't tell if it was amused or annoyed or something in between. "Because the world is wide, I suppose," Ylfing said. "Because there are beautiful things in it. Because there are... things no one knows about."

"You want to know them?"

"If no one knows them, *can* they be known?" Another little silence, and then Ylfing said in a quieter voice, "I think I'd like to try, though. Sometimes striving is reward enough itself, isn't it?"

Eisl wasn't sure about all that, but he hummed in vague acknowledgment. "You won't find any of that up here, you know. Things that no one knows. There's nothing like that on the ledge. No new stories either," he added, surprising himself when his voice came out unexpectedly bitter. "It's all—old news. Dullness. Sameness. Every day."

"I don't know about all that," Ylfing said. "*You* don't seem dull at all, for one thing."

"Thank you," Eisl said awkwardly. He might not himself be dull, but he was steeped in it—he breathed it and ate it and lived in the midst of it. "I'm sure you've met more interesting people in more interesting places."

"People are the same everywhere," Ylfing said solemnly, and then laughed to himself as if it was some kind of private joke.

"Are they? What do you mean?"

"I mean that people are people. You think, oh, the people who live there, on the other side of the world in that interesting place, they must be so interesting themselves—but then you go there and you meet them and they're... normal. They're just like the people you left behind—not in everything, of course. But there are people who are kind, and people who are cruel, and people who don't care one way or another. There are beautiful people and plain people. And it's usually in roughly the same proportions of one to the other." Eisl heard the hay rustle as Ylfing shifted again. "May I ask you something? Something about here?"

Eisl wondered what on earth Ylfing could have to ask questions of about anything on the ledge. It was just... the ledge. Plain, ordinary, mundane. "If you want to."

"The people down in the village—the town, that is— told me to come up here when I was asking around about… about one of the things no one knows, one of the things I'm looking for."

"Oh?"

"What's in the ravine, Eisl?"

WHEN EISL HAD BEEN ten years old, he'd gone to give offerings to the god of the ravine at midnight on midsummer, as the villagers of the Ledge did every year. He hadn't gone with the rest of them, not the whole laughing procession. Every year, they'd set up a bonfire near the entrance of the bridge, and they'd heat soup and cider to keep their bones warm—it was chilly at night in the mountains, even at midsummer—and they'd laugh and sing songs and take turns going out onto the bridge in ones or twos or small family groups to toss their offerings into the ravine and make wishes to the god who lived in it.

Most folks seemed to wish for a good harvest, or better weather (more rain, if it had been dry; less rain, if it had been wet), or a happy marriage, or healthy children, or safety in the mines, or for a sickly goat or its kid to recover and grow strong.

Eisl hated the midsummer offerings—some years, his parents had forced him to go to the party, to participate in the community. But they never forced him out onto the bridge, and they had taken it upon themselves to toss in an extra honey-cake on his behalf.

But that year, the summer he'd been twelve, he'd gone by himself, shuddering with fear as he crept through the woods and up to the edge of the ravine. He'd intended to stay fifteen feet back or so, but some of the other children had made fun of him for his fear, and he was aching to prove them wrong, at least to prove to *himself* that he wasn't afraid, even if they never found out what he had done.

He had forced himself almost to the edge—close enough to peer down into the dark abyss and see the river sparkling below. At midnight on midsummer, both moons were full and directly overhead, so the moonlight blazed down and made the landscape almost as bright as it was just before dawn. On any other night, you couldn't really see colors in the moonlight, only shades of black and blueish grey. But on midsummer—and midwinter, and the two equinoxes—the four times a year when the moons were both full at the same time, then it was bright enough to see colors, just barely. And so Eisl had seen the eerie blue-white mist rising from the roaring river below, the way it danced and twisted in the moonlight almost like a person... The way it had paused, and then the way it had *turned towards him.*

He had thought, just for a moment, that it was looking at him.

He'd heard the voice in his head. *Ah, hello, love—it's been a while, hasn't it?*

If he'd had his slingshot to hand, he would have slung a rock at the thing instantly, before he'd been able to think about it. All he'd had was a fragment of honeycake, crushed in his palm against a lump of goat cheese. He'd flung that instead, and then he'd turned tail and *run*.

"**W**HAT DO YOU MEAN?" Eisl's voice shook.

"The people in town told me that there was a spirit who lived in the ravine here," Ylfing said. "They said it's... not always a nice spirit. They said you give offerings to it and pray to it."

"Pray? What's pray?"

"Praying is—it's like talking, and wishing. It's when you talk to a god or a spirit or maybe just yourself, or maybe the whole world, and you ask for something you want, or for something bad to not happen."

"I guess some people make wishes," Eisl said, uncomfortable and longing more than anything that they could return to the warm drowsiness in the aftermath of pleasure. He felt rather cold now, and terribly awake. He shivered. "I don't. I don't... talk to it. The spirit, or whatever. The god. It's a god, or that's what people say."

"Can you tell me more? Where do they go to talk to it? Is there a shrine or a temple, or—"

Eisl didn't know what a temple was, but he'd heard people talking about shrines a little ways down the mountain path, shrines to other gods, lowland gods. On the ledge, there was just the ravine. "They go out onto the bridge. Nowhere else. They don't... talk to it every day. But when you do talk to it, you have to go out onto the bridge, that's what they said. Or at least... nearby." He swallowed hard, shivering.

"How near?"

"Near enough to see the water." No, that wasn't right. "The—the mist, I mean."

"The mist from the river and the cascades?"

"Yes. Well—not the normal mist, I don't think. The blue dancing mist."

Ylfing was quiet for a moment. "Can you tell me more about that?"

"No. Not really. You can go see it for yourself. Or—anyone else can tell you. I wouldn't have very much to say. I don't go to the ravine. I don't... look down there."

"I have asked other people," Ylfing said. "Nobody else mentioned blue dancing mist. They said that on midsummer's night, they give the spirit gifts of cakes and cheese and whatever other offerings they have."

"Well, the—the mist is probably so normal to them they just didn't notice it. Or mention it."

"But you did." He heard Ylfing shift closer, felt Ylfing's hand on his cheek, in his hair. "You said you don't look down—how did you see the mist?"

"I—I looked down once when I was small, the first time I crossed the bridge. Someone carried me; they carried me back across too, but that time I hid my face and cried the whole time. And then when I was twelve, I looked again." His voice dropped to a whisper. "I wanted to be brave."

"You were brave to look, if you were afraid." Ylfing stroked his hair, rubbed his thumb across Eisl's cheekbone, pulled him close when he felt Eisl trembling. Eisl buried his face against Ylfing's warm damp chest and shuddered again. "Can you tell me what you saw? Can you tell me about the mist?"

"Not much," said Eisl. "Why? Why do you want to know?"

"No one knows this but you, Eisl," Ylfing said, a little coaxing. "I'm looking for things no one knows. I—" He paused. Eisl felt Ylfing shake himself and when he spoke again his voice was different, more real, more... him. "I— sorry, I don't want to do that to get you to tell me." He took a deep breath. "I was taught things, by my master-Chant, who I was apprenticed to. He taught me how to winkle stories out of people, even hidden ones or secret ones that they might not otherwise want to share with an outsider." He kissed Eisl's hair, breathed again. "I'm not going to do that to you," he said, his voice firm—almost as if he were saying it aloud for *himself*, rather than so Eisl would know. "It sounds like this might be something you've never told anyone. If you don't want to tell me, you don't have to. But if you would like to, I would be grateful. It would... help me."

"With what?"

"I'm looking for something. Someone." Ylfing paused; Eisl might have spoken again, filled the silence, except he could sense somehow that Ylfing wasn't done speaking, that he only needed a moment more to get his thoughts in order. "Once—recently, only about a year ago—a god looked at me. Spoke to me. He came to me in dreams, but I lost the thread of our connection just as I realized what was happening. It snapped, or wore out. I thought it was only dreams at first, you know. I didn't recognize him."

"Why would you recognize him?"

"I'd heard stories about him. He's the god of the ancient Chants and their people, who came over the sea thousands of years ago when their homeland sank beneath the waves."

Eisl shivered, thinking of the god in the ravine... "He came into your dreams?"

"Yes."

"He spoke to you?"

Ylfing hesitated. "No. No, he was quiet. He might have... said my name? I can't remember now. I might have just imagined that, later on. Wishful thinking, you know. No, he was silent most of the time. He gestured a little, I suppose. That counts as speaking sometimes. But not enough for me to... know anything about what he meant or what he wanted."

"The god of the ravine spoke to me," Eisl whispered.

"What? Did he? What did he say? What did it sound like?" Ylfing took a deep breath. "You don't have to tell me anything, but... I don't even know what I don't know. I don't know what will help. If there's anything you feel like telling me..."

"It's frightening. The ravine god. It's... it's not human. I don't think it thinks in the same way humans do, but it was still able to look into my head and—speak to me."

"What did it say?" Ylfing breathed.

"'Long time no see', basically."

"Has anyone else spoken to him? Do you know?"

Eisl shifted, shivered, patted around in the straw for his tunic and sat up to pull it over his head. "In stories, I guess. They're—I'm not good at telling stories, I'm not like you. They're about the god granting wishes, or growing angry."

"What does it become angry about?"

"I don't know. The stories don't say. They just say things like 'Long and long ago, when our grandfathers' grandfathers were living on the ledge, there came a day when the god in the ravine grew angry.' That sort of thing. So we give it offerings. Honey cakes and cheese and things. Sometimes someone goes down to the village and brings up something nicer if they have a wish they really want granted."

"Does that help? Does it keep the god from growing angry?"

"I don't know. Maybe. Maybe not."

"What does he do when he's angry? Avalanches? Landslides?"

Eisl shuddered at the very thought. "No. He breaks the bridge, or knocks people off of it. Or he makes so much mist that you can't see your own feet. In the stories, that's what it says, anyway. In all the time I've been alive, I don't think I've ever heard of it getting angry." He paused, a distant memory swimming to the surface of his brain like a silvery darting minnow. "I think... a year or two before I was born, there might have been something that happened. That was the last time the bridge broke, anyway. People are better now about keeping an eye on it and checking it for worn bits that need to be repaired."

"What about things in the village, does it do anything here when it gets angry?"

"No... No, just the ravine and a bit of the edges."

"What about wishes?"

"It only grants wishes if you're standing on the bridge. In the stories, that's what they say."

"Ah. So perhaps it's that the god can't reach beyond the ravine at all."

Eisl had a hard time wrapping his mind around that. The god seemed so... powerful, so frightening—how could it be that it couldn't reach beyond the ravine? "I don't know... I said it wasn't human and probably doesn't think like humans do. Maybe it just doesn't care about anything beyond the ravine. I don't know that it makes sense to think of what... of what *people* would do."

"You don't think a god is a person?"

"Maybe *yours* is. You saw him in dreams, you would have been able to see whether he was a person or not. I haven't seen the god in the ravine. Just... blue dancing mist, like I said."

"Hm..." After a moment, Ylfing stroked his hair again. "Who was in charge of fixing the bridge the last time it broke?"

"A bunch of people, I guess. Not really a one-person job. Everybody helps out when things like that happen. If one of the mine shafts collapses, or if they break into a pocket of bad air while they're down there... Or if the bridge breaks. Or if a storm comes and knocks a tree onto someone's house."

"So if I ask people of your parents' generation? They will know? They might have worked on the bridge?"

Eisl shrugged. "Probably. Helping with the bridge doesn't always mean actually doing things *with* the bridge. Sometimes it means watching the children, or cooking for the workers. But if they didn't touch the bridge themselves, they would have known who did."

"All right. Thank you, Eisl."

Eisl turned towards him blindly in the dark, drawing closer to Ylfing's soft warmth. "Tell me a story. To make up for—for talking about all that."

Ylfing's hand carded through his hair and he pulled Eisl's face to pillow against his shoulder, kissing his forehead. "What story shall I tell you? What would you like to hear about?"

Eisl closed his eyes tight against the dark. "Somewhere far away," he whispered. "Somewhere very far away from here. Somewhere with no mountains and —and no ledge, and no ravine."

"No mountains, no ledge, no ravine," Ylfing murmured. "Let me think, then... Once, when I was still an apprentice, my master-Chant and I were traveling across the Sea of Sun, the great desert. You remember, I told you about deserts." Eisl nodded. "We were staying with a man called Pashafi, who was a man of one of the Ondoro tribes. They live in walking huts that scuttle across the sand like beetles. They keep goats too, you know, just like you—but their goats are bigger, with much shorter coats, and very long ears. Amazingly velvety and soft, those ears, just beautiful—but the goats look a little funny."

"All goats look funny," Eisl said, relaxing against Ylfing slowly.

"That's true. They all have odd little faces, but I thought these goats looked odder than most. They have bright blue-white eyes—that's the thing that makes them look oddest, I think. Blue-white eyes and long, long velvet ears. Pashafi told me their ears help keep them cool in the desert. The Ondoro build their huts so that they have a little fenced area underneath, and as the huts move, the goats move with it."

"What if they get tired?" Eisl said, already beginning to feel drowsy.

"Ah, that was my first question too, when I saw the huts—but these odd-looking goats are as nimble as any other breed, you see. There are a few little platforms suspended underneath the huts, so any goat that gets tired can hop up onto it to rest, or if someone needs to go down to tend to them, they can sit there and watch over them." Ylfing stroked his hair slowly, slowly, gently... "Perhaps another day, I would tell you why the goats walk on the sand while the people almost never do. But I think today you'd prefer to hear about lovely things instead—like the colors of the sky at dawn just before the sun rises over the desert..."

THE NEXT DAY, EISL rose at dawn as usual to attend to the goats and drive them up to the pasture. He sat in the sun and whittled—just little pieces that someone would take down to the town to trade on some market day. Everyone on the ledge had some little task they did to keep their hands busy, and nearly everything they produced went to the town's market and was turned into coins to buy supplies, stores for the winter, new seed crops, a new billy goat every now and then to keep the bloodlines varied...

Eisl's hands knew their business, even if his mind was wandering.

He kept thinking of the night before, of what it was like to be *kissed*, to be pressed back into the warm, sweet-smelling hay...

He wished that was the only thing his mind was lingering on. He wished it would have strayed no farther than that. Ylfing—or Chant, or whatever his name was, Eisl couldn't remember which was which today—had asked too many questions about the ravine, and it had made all Eisl's hair stand on end.

That was the trouble with living on the ledge. There was no escape from the ravine—it was always there. Tight on the edge of the world, as far as he was concerned. Right on the edge of his mind, so he was always... well, on edge.

He thought, not for the first time, that if he could only work up the courage to *cross,* then he would be free. He could go down to the town and never see the ravine again, except off in the distance whenever he looked up to the mountains above. He could... go farther than that, and never see it again at all. He could run off into *Ylfing's* world, which was broader and brighter and rich with all manner of things. He could find a place where no one knew about the ravine or its god.

Part of him was as terrified of that as he was of the ravine itself. He set down the butter knife he was whittling and looked off to the horizon, the winding river and the field and the little roads... He knew the world was bigger than the Ledge, of course. But it had never seemed all *that* big from his vantage point in the goat pasture. With the prospect of going out into it, though, with the prospect of *seeing* it... He felt very, very small, suddenly. The roads below were hair-fine threads, and he had sometimes glimpsed specks on them—people walking, or a horse and rider, or a wagon... A speck. That's what he'd be if he went out.

But here on the ledge, he was... confined. Confined, without option to leave as long as he was too afraid to cross the bridge.

Perhaps there was some other option. Some middle option. If he could manage to cross the ravine—all the grandest possibilities began with crossing the ravine—

then he wouldn't necessarily have to go out into the world as Ylfing did. He wouldn't have to see all of it, nor go *very* far. He wouldn't have to go see a desert or the sea —he could build a house on the other side of the ravine, maybe. He could be the one that the villagers of the ledge sent down to the market with their goods for trade, and then he could get a taste of the world—just a taste— before coming almost all the way home. The others had no such fear of the ravine; his friends and family would cross over to visit him. Perhaps they would help him clear another field, and they'd take the goats across the bridge so that he could continue herding them, if going to the market proved as terrifying as crossing the ravine did. (But how could anything be as terrifying as crossing the ravine?)

At evening as the sun set behind the crag, Eisl drove the goats home and went looking for Ylfing. He found him at Pollot's again, this time talking to Granny Adelin, who served as herbwoman, midwife, and medic to both the people and the animals on the ledge. She was ancient and as weathered as the mountain face, but not so old that her mind had yet begun to go.

Eisl sidled up to the table; Ylfing looked up and smiled and nodded to a chair—*not* interrupting Granny Adelin's mutterings. Eisl knew she hated when people did that. He knew everything about everyone in this damned village.

"Four times we had to fix that bridge," she was saying. "Four times in four days, 'til folk started getting nervous and desperate and trying stupider things than honey-cakes and cheese." She snorted and glanced at Eisl as he sat down. "This one's mother was just starting to swell in the stomach around that time. She wasn't from the ledge, you know. Town girl this one's father fell in love with, thought herself a clever sort. Used to read *books*." Granny Adelin snorted again. "What call anybody has for book-learnin' on the ledge, I couldn't say. Everything you'd need to know is already known by somebody. Anyhow, Marin went out to the ravine one night, the night after the half-fixed bridge had collapsed again, and the next morning the work wasn't touched and folks finished up fixing the bridge and young Marin was as smug as a cat in the creampot. Told me she was gonna come to me in a couple days to get rid of her stomach, and could I have the herbs ready. 'Course I was surprised, 'cause she and Leric seemed like they were happy newlyweds who'd be happier with a full crib, but —" Adelin held up both her hands, shaking her head. "I don't ask questions when girls want their belly gone —'cept occasionally things like, 'Do we need to do something about that husband of yours?' Only if he's a problem, though." She lowered her hands and shrugged. "Village this small, usually it doesn't get to that point. A man gets troublesome, all the other men tell him to get himself straight. No room for that shit on the Ledge. It's a hard enough life up here as it is without people throwing tantrums and getting mean for no reason. Still, sometimes you get a goat who goes bad, so you cull it; sometimes you get a *man* who goes bad... Anyhow, she came to me a couple days later, still pleased with herself —little chit—and I gave her the herbs to get rid of her stomach, and we sat down to knit and chat and wait it out." Adelin took a long gulp of beer from her cup. "Didn't work," she said with a smack of her lips. "Didn't think anything of it—sometimes you get a girl with a constitution like granite and it takes a couple tries to get things moving. Didn't work the next five times either, and then I told her that the baby might as well be stuck in there with pine resin. She was upset by then—not about the baby, which I thought was odd. Usually girls cry when things like that don't go the way they want it to, but Marin was *mad*. Kept going on about how she needed *this* baby out of her so that she could start in on another one."

"Why?" Ylfing asked.

Eisl was... He was... He didn't know how to feel. He'd never heard this story, *never*, not from his parents, not from Granny Adelin, not from anyone else.

"Well, she said she'd told that thing in the ravine that it could have the baby growing in her belly if it'd play nice and stop messing with the bridge," Adelin said evenly. "Ooh, how I whapped that little fool upside the head! I asked what she thought she was doing, and she said she said it were obvious, and I said it weren't and that she ought to explain, and she said she was gonna get emptied out and then take all the bloody cloths and bundle it all up and toss it in the ravine. Marin said she'd been *real careful* not to say 'my firstborn'—but it didn't matter. The thing wanted *that* baby. I told her I weren't going to be responsible for helping her cheat her way out of her promise, not to that thing in the ravine— but I showed her what the herbs look like and where to find them in the forest and how to prepare them, because I'm not about to keep back useful knowledge from a girl who's trying to make choices, but that's as far as I went. Gave her the tools and the know-how and said the rest of it was on her own head. Don't know if she tried any more times, nor how many." Adelin clucked her tongue. "Never got called in to nurse her through it, though, and every time I saw her, she was still increasing. Easy birth it was, too, in the end, easiest I've ever been to. When they called me up to say it was her time, I had a feeling it was going to be an odd one, so I scuttled over as quick as my legs could go. Twas a lucky thing I did, too—I barely got there in time to catch." She took another long draft of beer. "All credit to the thing in the ravine, it *did* do a damn good job. Thorough, like. You don't expect a thing to be that thorough, you know? Sure, keeping the babe safe in the belly, that's one thing, but making sure it gets born safe too—safe *and* easy to boot. Marin weren't even in much pain! Barely sweating, when I got there, and I only heard her groan once. I think that was from effort, though, not from hurting. *Eerie* birth that was." She eyed Eisl. "Grew into an eerie boy, too, didn't you?"

He didn't reply.

"What happened after that?" Ylfing said. "Did she... try to give him to the thing?"

Adelin sipped her beer, studying him over the rim. "Don't know," she said after a long moment. "Heard someone saw her go down the path to the bridge that very night—on her own feet and all! That thing sure knows what it's doing with childbirth—but I don't ask questions, and when I stopped by the next day to check on her and the babe, she had roses in her cheeks like a fresh spring morning, and he was suckling like a hungry calf. And then he just kept being there, bigger every time I saw him, and the bridge hasn't broken in... must be twenty years now, mustn't it?"

"And you think it's because of that thing in the ravine?"

"Don't know, do I? We give it offerings and some folk are brave enough to make wishes to it, and some years that worked and some years it didn't. All I know is that Marin talked to the thing, and that Eisl is an odd one."

She eyed Eisl again. "Oughta talk to the odd one if you want odd sorts of answers."

"I've never heard about any of this," Eisl rasped. "I didn't know. I don't know anything."

"Mm," said Adelin, clearly unconvinced. "A person always knows more'n they think they do, as I sees it."

"DO YOU WANT TO talk about it?" Ylfing said, linking their arms together as they walked out into the dark. The sky was still bright overhead, purple streaked with faint wisps of pink-orange clouds. Sunset, at least elsewhere in the world. Eisl had never seen a sunset. There wasn't a path to the other side of the mountain, unless you climbed up a couple sheer cliff faces and hiked around to the other side on scree and rocks that even a goat might think twice about. The other side of the mountain was the only place the sunset would be visible without... without crossing the ravine.

"I don't know," Eisl said. He felt... hollow. Restless. A little bit like crying, or tearing his hair and shouting in frustration. "Tell me—tell me what you do. Tell me about the world again."

Ylfing opened his mouth, probably to ask what sort of story Eisl wanted to hear about, and then he paused. His expression became sober, steady, a little sad, a little wary. "Why do you ask?"

"I want—I want to—" His heart thundered in his chest. "I don't want to be here anymore," he burst out. "I don't *want to be here*."

"Do you have family here?"

"Cousins. My uncle and aunt. That's it." His mother had died of pneumonia when he was twelve; his father two years ago, when a mine shaft collapse had left him addled in the mind from lack of air before he'd slipped away quietly in his sleep several weeks later. Cousins, uncle and aunt, the villagers—yes, there were people he cared about. But there was also the ravine, and the constant fear and discomfort.

"Do you want to leave because you feel like you don't belong?" Ylfing asked gently.

Eisl closed his eyes and breathed in the damp mountain air. "I don't know what that means. I've never —it's not about belonging or not. I'm... made of this place. I've lived here all my life, I've only stepped foot off the ledge once. My lungs have always been full of this air, my ears have always been full of the sound of the river in the ravine, my belly has always been filled with the food grown here. The dirt is on my hands and under my feet. It's not about belonging."

"Because belonging means ownership? And you don't feel like this place owns you—just that it *is* you."

"As the mountain is the rocks, yes."

"Why do you want to leave?" Ylfing asked gently.

"I can go if I want to," Eisl replied, more impatiently than was necessary. "If I can get across the bridge, I can go anywhere. Away from here." An ache settled in his chest. "I don't *want* to be made just of this place, just these rocks and this air and the food grown on these mountainsides. I don't want to be so... *small.*"

Ylfing's kind expression softened further, almost to the point of relenting. "You are not small, Eisl. Even if you stayed here for your whole life, that doesn't make you small."

"It *does.* It does. I'm—I'm trapped here. I don't want to be trapped, I don't want to stay here, I don't want to be anchored to one spot for always and forever, I want to— to *go.*"

"You know that if you go, you're allowed to turn back, don't you? You're always allowed to go home, if you decide you want to."

"I won't want to," Eisl said recklessly. "I won't. How could I miss anything so boring? How could I care when there's everything else out there?"

Ylfing studied him. After a long moment he said, "Are you asking me to take you as an apprentice, or just a traveling companion?"

Caught by surprise, Eisl laughed aloud. "Apprentice? We're the same age, or nearly so! Wouldn't that be odd?"

"Yes," Ylfing said steadily. "But Chants are odd."

"I don't need to be a Chant or whatever," Eisl said. "That's your thing, I don't need to horn in on it."

Ylfing paused just at the cliff edge of relenting. "Are you sure? You won't change your mind later? I wouldn't mind a traveling companion, but I don't want an apprentice." He shuddered. "At least not yet. Not for a long time, probably. So if you change your mind later... I don't want an apprentice, do you understand?"

"Yes, that's fine, that's fine! I don't want that either, I don't even really know what a Chant is other than a storyteller, I just want—*out there.*"

Ylfing nodded slowly. "All right."

Eisl's heart lifted. "Yeah? Really? When can we leave? Soon?"

Ylfing looked around at the town, looked off in the direction of the ravine, sighed. "Yes, soon. I want to stay another day or two, just to be sure, but... I don't think this is going to turn out to be part of what I was looking for. And you'll need time to pack and say goodbye to everyone." He fixed that kind expression on Eisl again— so kind, so very kind, heartwrenchingly kind, almost like he had enough benevolence and warmth in his heart to blanket the entire world with it. "You can change your mind whenever you want," he said again. "You can turn back *whenever you want.*"

But how could Eisl turn back? He couldn't think of anything that would make him want to turn back, once he got free and got out.

His heart sang; his spirit felt light and joyous. He remembered, in a rush of glorious sense-memory, going down the forest-lined pathway to the town with his parents for that market day long ago. He wondered if it was the same as it had been then, if it still smelled of pine and sunshine and summer, if the light still came through the trees in the late afternoon...

He could find out. He didn't have to simply wonder—he could find out. He was going to find out.

H E SPENT THE NEXT few days as Ylfing had suggested—he went around to all the villagers and told them he was going away. They were stunned, confused. Some of them laughed; some of them shook their heads.

Ylfing spoke to the villagers too, but every time Eisl overheard something, it was them telling stories to him, rather than the other way around. He got them to tell him everything about life on the Ledge; he must have heard all the major gossip of the last fifty years; he got them to teach him songs... Not songs that Eisl thought were worth anything, nothing that seemed like someone who had seen the entire world would care about. It was simple, common, mundane stuff. Songs for milking and sowing and reaping, songs for kneading bread and churning butter, songs to sing over the new beer when it was poured into kegs and rolled into a chamber near the entrance of the mines to ferment. Songs to sing as they hung the cheeses in their cloths in the caves too, which the old folks said would ward off bugs and bats and all manner of unpleasant things.

Ylfing listened to them all, learned them all, sang them back to make sure he had them word-perfect, listened as the villagers bickered about what the right verses were. Learned those verses too. He had a fine voice, smooth and bright and a little sad, the sort of voice that people stopped to listen to when he sang, that brought tears into their eyes if the song was even the slightest bit sad or slow.

Ylfing didn't ask about the god of the ravine anymore. Eisl was far too busy making the rounds to pay any heed anyway, telling everyone that he was going and he would never cross to this side of the bridge ever again, not ever.

He was impatient; he was nearly hopping with impatience by the time he crawled into bed the night before they were to leave. He had spent an exhilarating hour or two kissing Ylfing up against the back of his uncle's barn, catching him around the waist and lifting him off his feet—he was lean and rangy, almost scrawny, and Eisl could have sworn he didn't weigh much more than a goat did, and had told him so.

Ylfing, already laughing from being swept up, had laughed harder, laughed until Eisl had set him down and pushed him up against the barn again and kissed him. Eisl had thought of nights on the road with him and all the other places he might kiss him—or someone else, or as many people as he liked, because the world was *full* of people and Eisl was going to go and *see*.

He fell asleep with that precious thought ringing in his heart and in his mind. He was going to go and see.

E ISL HEAVED HIS BAG onto his shoulder—it weighed approximately as much as a goat, or Ylfing —and kissed the cheeks of his aunt and uncle and cousins as they watched in dubious disbelief.

"Be safe, lad," his aunt said, her voice quavering a little. "Come back and visit every now and then. I know it's a long walk up from the town, but a couple times a year would be nice."

He hadn't quite been able to make her understand that he was going far, far beyond the town. He kissed her cheek again. "Anytime I'm within a day's walk, I'll come, auntie. At least to the other side of the bridge." But who knew how long it would be until that happened? From everything Ylfing had said, the world seemed much bigger than a day's walking would take him.

He met up with Ylfing at what passed for the center square of the village, which was really just a mid-sized clear area in front of Pollot's. Ylfing had a bag at his feet, which he picked up and slung over his shoulder when he saw Eisl approaching—it was significantly smaller and lighter than Eisl's own. "Ready?" Ylfing said.

Eisl nodded, his heart in his throat.

Without another word, they... went. Through the winding little path through the pines to the bridge, the ravine; the roar of the river got loader as they approached.

Eisl's heart beat faster, skittering in his chest like a frightened animal; his breath came short, his mouth felt dry.

Ylfing went to the edge of the ravine, twenty or so feet from the entrance to the bridge. Eisl hung back a little— he'd forgotten this part. Or rather, he hadn't forgotten it, but it had been drowned out in all the excitement of packing and dreaming of the open road and the wide world out there *beyond* the impossible challenge of the bridge itself.

"I heard stories about you in the village," Ylfing whispered. "The one down the mountain, and the one here on the ledge. I thought—hoped—that you might have been mine, but it seems that you're not."

Eisl could barely hear him over the rush of the water. He glanced nervously down into the ravine as far as he could see—there was no strange blue mist today, just the rising vapor from the river and the cascade. "What," he said, his voice cracking. "What are you doing? Are you praying?"

"I suppose I am," Ylfing said quietly. "I was just... speaking to whatever or whoever is down there. I don't know if it—or he—could hear me."

"You're not going to make a wish, are you?" Eisl asked, nervous. He took another step back from the edge, feeling faintly sick.

"No. No, I'm not going to make a wish. I don't know enough about him; I fear even a kindly god might find a stranger making requests to be presumptuous." He sighed and turned. "I pray to my own feet, I suppose, when I pray at all. They've carried me here from half the world away, and with luck they'll carry me half the world further. I pray for good roads and good weather and the kindness of strangers and fellow travelers met in those places between places." Ylfing looked up at the sky. He seemed very far away suddenly. "And that the open road will lead me to the threshold of my great mystery, and that the good weather and kind strangers will hurry my journey rather than hinder it." He looked at Eisl and smile ruefully. "You come up with all kinds of poetic nonsense when you've been walking on your own for long enough. Don't mind me." He nodded at the ground.

"Pick out a little rock. Small enough to hold in your palm."

"And do what with it?" He hoped the answer wasn't *hurl it into the ravine.* They threw offerings down there; throwing rocks seemed... impolite. Provocative. Asking for trouble.

"Put it in your bag and take it with you."

"Is this some kind of Chant thing?" Eisl said, kneeling to pick up a small flat rock near his foot.

"Not really. More of a *me* thing. I think it's good luck. And you might one day appreciate having a piece of home in your pocket."

He cast another long, wistful look down into the ravine and walked along the edge to the bridge. Eisl followed, his rock clutched in his hand.

Just as Ylfing set foot on the bridge, he turned to glance back at Eisl. He paused, frowned. "Are you all right?"

The *yes* evaporated in Eisl's mouth.

"I don't know," he said, his voice shaking. "I don't know."

He met Ylfing's eyes—he looked sad and benevolent and painfully understanding. "You don't have to go," he said. "You don't have to."

Eisl said, in a voice so small that he couldn't even convince himself, "But I want to."

Ylfing just stood there, one foot on the bridge. Looking at him.

Eisl trembled, tried to straighten his shoulders, exhaled all his terror, and took another step closer.

A moment later, he found himself on the ground, fallen to his knees, emotion welling up in him. "I can't," he choked out. "I can't, I can't, I can't. I want to—Ylfing, I want to, I *want to*, please make me. Drag me across, please."

Ylfing looked at him—so sad, so very sad—and Eisl knew what he would say before he said it.

"I'm sorry," Ylfing whispered, the sorrow piercing in his eyes.

"You—" Eisl stared at him, shocked, *betrayed.*

"Please don't look at me like that."

"You're just going to leave me here, aren't you?"

Ylfing squatted beside him and brushed Eisl's hair out of his face. He tipped Eisl's face up and pressed a brief dry kiss to his mouth. "It's your choice, Eisl."

"But I'm choosing to go!" Eisl cried, tears spilling over and running hot down his cheeks. "I want to go!"

"Then come. But if you're not ready, then I can't stay and wait until you are. I'm sorry—I have my own answers to seek." Ylfing kissed him again, still chaste, cupping Eisl's face between two hands. "I can't force you to come with me. I won't. I know you want me to, but *I can't do that for you.* One day, you'll have the courage to cross. I promise you that this is true. One day you'll be ready. There's no shame that today isn't that day."

Eisl pushed Ylfing's hands away, suddenly furious. "You're not *listening to me!* I want to leave!"

"All right," Ylfing said, still so painfully kind and sad. "I'm going to cross the bridge, Eisl. You can follow me if you want to. And if you're not ready, I can't make you be ready. I'm sorry."

"Don't—don't go, please don't go—" A moment ago he had pushed off Ylfing's hands; now he reached for them, frightened and alone. "Take me with you."

"I can't," Ylfing said softly as he stood. "I'm sorry. I can't take you with me; you have to follow of your own free will or not at all."

"Ylfing!"

"I hope I'll see you on the other side," Ylfing said, stepping away and pausing again at the entrance to the bridge. "And if I don't—I'm sorry our paths diverged so soon. If you're able to follow me later... Well, I'm going to be staying in the town tonight, and then I'm heading south as much as possible." He gave Eisl a bracing smile. "Good luck. I'm sorry."

"It's just the crossing!" Eisl shouted, tears spilling down his cheeks. "Just help me cross!"

Ylfing hesitated. "I'll watch from the other side. I'll watch, and if you get stuck partway across, I'll come back and help you the rest of the way. That's the most

I'm willing to do. I cannot risk you feeling later like I pushed you into it—I can't do that to you. I need *you* to know in the future that it was your choice to leave or to stay, not mine."

He held Eisl's gaze for another few long moments—Eisl couldn't find anything else to say. He just looked at Ylfing, pleading, crying out with anger and frustration and fear in his heart...

Ylfing nodded a little, regretful, and turned away. He crossed the bridge, not looking down, not even looking aside. Just... walked, like it was nothing. Like he was keeping his eyes fixed on his own goal, far off on the other side of that bridge. Far off on the other side of the world. They were one and the same, or they might as well have been.

Just as he'd promised, Ylfing stepped off the bridge on the other side and turned back. He stood there, watching, one hand around the strap of his bag on his shoulder.

Eisl swallowed the dryness from his mouth and forced his trembling body to its feet. He took several shuddering steps towards the bridge—he even managed to get his hand on the post, and then—

He couldn't. He couldn't.

Fear swept over him and pushed him back from the bridge, dropped him to his knees in the dirt. Despair and anger overwhelmed him.

He screamed and slapped his hands on the ground, tore out chunks of grass and dirt with his hands, tossed his bag aside, buried his face in his grubby hands, yelled all his rage again until it drained out of him and he was left sobbing with fury and disappointment.

When next he raised his head, he expected Ylfing to be gone, but he was still standing there, still watching. Eisl stared at him dully, his cheeks wet and muddy, his heart aching in his chest. As he watched, Ylfing raised a hand, waved to him a little. Laid his hand over his heart, as if to say sorry. He was too far away for Eisl to see his expression clearly, but he saw Ylfing open his mouth to shout something—the roar of the river below was too loud, and it drowned out everything but the barest suggestion of words that Eisl couldn't make out.

He got up without another gesture or look toward Ylfing, collected his bag with shaking hands, and turned away. It felt like dying, a little—turning away from life and going back to dull monotonous existence.

He only made it twenty feet or so down the forest path before he stumbled to a stop again, aching and aching and *aching* with the wrenching disappointment, with loss—with *grief,* that's what it was. Grief for the life he'd just given up by turning away.

Eisl didn't want to go back. He couldn't bear to go back. And yet he couldn't make himself go onward; he didn't have the strength or the courage for it. He was trapped now, trapped between two sheer cliffs, neither of which could be climbed. Trapped in a narrow space the same width as the ravine.

He turned back again, went back to the edge of the forest and stopped. Ylfing had gone. Eisl wasn't surprised.

He sat on the ground, hugged his bag in his lap, stared at the bridge. He couldn't. He had to. But he couldn't.

He sat there for the rest of the morning and most of the afternoon, until someone came up the path and exclaimed in surprise at the sight of him. One of the villagers, he saw, looking up. He shook his head, refused to respond or even listen to anything the woman said. She tried to kneel beside him and wipe the tears and dirt from his face; he pushed her hands away. She tried to tug him up by his arm; he yanked it out of her grip and hugged his bag tighter, burying his face against it.

Eventually, she left.

Others came—she must have told someone. Eisl kept his face buried against his bag, his eyes scrunched tight. He shook off all attempts to help him, slapped away the hands that petted his hair or squeezed his shoulder. Ignored everything they said to him.

They left too, eventually.

When Eisl lifted his head again, the light had gone except for the sunset colors in the sky. He looked around and found that someone had left a plate of food for him.

Bread, cheese, stew that had gone cold and gummy. He stared at it for a long moment, picked it up, and hurled it with all his might into the ravine.

He ate the food he'd packed in his bag instead—Ylfing had shown him how to make journey-cakes with oats and nuts and honey. It was cloyingly sweet and sticky, and his mouth was too dry to chew it easily—he hadn't realized how thirsty he was. He didn't have a waterskin; Ylfing had said they could buy one down in the town.

Eisl got up and stomped along the edge of the forest until he found a clear spot just within the treeline. He wrapped his cloak around himself, laid on the ground thick with last year's half-decayed leaves, pillowed his head on his bag, and tried to sleep.

It was cold, even for a summer night. The mist rising from the ravine chilled the air and the roar of the river was louder here, but he was so accustomed to it that he barely heard it or felt it. He could have gone back to his uncle's house, slept in his own warm bed.

But then no, of course he couldn't.

He refused to think of anything; he kept his mind empty of thought as much as possible. He slept, chilled to the bone but in no danger of freezing. He could have lit a fire if he'd cared to.

He had no dreams that night, and he woke in the morning feeling no better and no less trapped.

He went back to the bridge, because he had to. There was no other choice. He shook with fear as he approached, but he managed to get all the way up to the entrance and put his hands on the posts of the gate that anchored the suspension ropes on this side. He stood there, bracing himself, his fingernails digging into the wood as he forced himself to stand and look out over the bridge, the ravine...

If he could cross, Ylfing would still be in town. Eisl could make it down the mountain path by midday or early afternoon if he hurried—enough time to catch up with him, even if he'd only just left. Someone would have seen him. They could point Eisl in the right direction.

He put his foot out on the bridge, one step.

A flash of blue in the corner of his eye, a twist of something that might have been dancing mist brought another sickening wave of fear into his throat and he stumbled back again, shoving himself away from the gate and shuddering. He turned away and staggered on shaky legs to the treeline, managing four or five steps before he collapsed, weak and faint.

He buried his face in his hands again, but he was too thirsty to cry, too angry at himself, at the ravine, at Ylfing...

No. It wasn't Ylfing's fault. They had made no promises to each other—they had only known each other for a few days. And Ylfing *had* said he was chasing his own mysteries. It wouldn't have been fair to expect Ylfing to take responsibility for him as if they were bound by the ties of friendship or kinship or love—it was only that he he'd been so different, so *strange,* and Eisl was so desperate...

The villagers came out to see him again—to see if he was still there, likely. They didn't try to talk to him. He saw it was his aunt, his cousin Lisen, a few others. His cousin put another plate of food on the ground beside him and stood up with her hands on her hips. "Are you going to stop this foolishness? Just come home."

His aunt shushed her as she placed a jug of water beside the plate. "Take your time, Eisl," she said, sighing a little as if he were a spoiled child in the midst of a tantrum. "Stay out as long as you want. I'll make your favorite for dinner tonight, if you like."

He took the jug, drank from it, eyed the plate of food.

"Where's the other plate?" Lisen huffed. "Where'd you put it?"

The way she said it—snobbish, irritated—annoyed him enough that without another thought he picked up today's plate and flung it into the ravine too.

"Eisl!" cried Lisen and his aunt.

"I don't know what's gotten into you!" his aunt said. "Really!"

"We should just let him starve out here," said Lisen, unusually vicious—she must have been one of the people trying to touch him and comfort him yesterday. He must have offended her, pushing her away like he had. She did have a tendency to hold grudges.

His aunt sighed. "There's food at home if you want it, Eisl. Please don't throw the jug in. Your father made that for me before you were born."

When he didn't answer, they left. Eisl drank the water, ate more of the journeycakes from his bag, stared stonily at the bridge.

He slept there again that night, in the forest on piles of leaves. He felt like he had been chilly for so long that he only vaguely remembered what it was like to be warm—but he'd had long cold days on the mountainside with the goats, and he knew what kind of cold was dangerous and what was merely uncomfortable.

He woke the next morning and stumbled out of the trees to the bridge. He sat on the ground at the gate and scooted closer, inch by inch, until he could put his hands on the support posts of the bridge again and slowly extend his legs out onto the planks. He was breathing hard, as if he'd run a race or carried goats one by one back down to the barn in a blizzard.

He made himself sit there and stare at the bridge. He listened to the creak of its ropes, the slight sway of it in the breeze, the thick mist rising up from below. His heart fluttered in his chest until he felt like he would have thrown up if he'd been any more afraid.

His aunt came alone around lunchtime with another plate of food. "Everyone told me I'm wasting my time," she said, standing over him. She sniffed. "You're too old to be behaving like this, Eisl. It's childish! You're a man grown—there's no call for you to be acting like this, throwing plates and shoving people and sulking." She paused, evidently waiting for him to have some kind of a response. He ignored her. "I'd like an apology," she said. "For the plates, and for your rude behavior."

He was silent. He stared at the bridge.

"Eisl, for goodness' sake!" she cried. "What's gotten into you! Just apologize and come home!"

He was silent. If he could just cross the bridge—if he could cross the bridge today, there was still a chance he could catch up with Ylfing. Someone would remember the young man with the pale hair and the astonishing blue eyes. Eisl could catch back up with him, *prove* that he'd meant what he said, and they could travel together... All he needed to do was cross.

He just needed to cross.

"Eisl," she said, cajoling now since scolding hadn't worked. "Eisl, it's been days, everyone thinks you've gone strange. You don't want them to think you've gone strange, do you? Look, I made you a pot pie—lovely and fresh. Partridge! Your uncle shot one yesterday, and I said to him, *Oh, Eisl loves a bit of partridge pie, doesn't he!*"

He said nothing.

She made a frustrated, hurt little noise and said, "I wish you'd listen to reason! Why won't you even speak to us? Eisl!"

He clenched his jaw and said nothing.

"Fine. Fine, whatever you're going through, I'm sure you'll come to your senses when you've eaten a bit and had time to think." She set the pie on the ground beside him—she'd used a plate to carry it, but the pie was wrapped in a cloth so that she could set it directly on the ground next to him and take the plate away, presumably so he wouldn't throw it into the ravine.

Without hesitation, he picked up the pie and threw that into the ravine anyway.

Eisl's aunt turned away without another word and stomped down the forest path. "Nothing tomorrow," she shouted over her shoulder. "Come home if you want to eat, otherwise stay out here and be hungry! See if I care!"

He was trembling again, but it was with anger again. And beyond anger, something else. Determination.

He got to his feet and gripped the two posts at the entrance of the bridge, slid his hands down to the rope railing tied to them, leaned out as far as he could and gripped the rope in both hands before he stepped... cautiously... forward.

I suppose you're not going to apologize to me either? Came a whispering voice in his head.

Eisl stumbled back, panting, and fell on his ass in the dirt, scrambling even further back.

I can't see you anymore, came the voice, now only a faint whisper—but unlike Ylfing's shout, it didn't get lost in the white roar of the river.

"Leave me alone," Eisl said, his voice shaking. "Leave me alone, let me cross. I just want to cross."

Come back to the edge, the voice—the *god*—murmured. *Perhaps we'll consider these three offerings your apology. There, now all is mended and we can be friends again, can't we.*

The voice was silky, beguiling—but it was speaking into the back of Eisl's mind and he felt sick with terror.

Ylfing's god hadn't killed him. Ylfing's god had come to him in dreams and had been interesting enough to send him running *towards* the god rather than *away from* him.

Eisl wanted badly to be away from this one. "Leave me alone. Leave me alone."

Why? said the god, almost plaintive. *You were given to me. A boy for a bridge, isn't that a fair bargain?*

Eisl shut his eyes tight and swallowed. "What do you want? Why me? Why—"

You knew what it was to be trapped, the god whispered. *Even then, even before your soul had a body to inhabit. You were tied to her, waiting for her body to finish making another for you, and you were trapped. Don't you remember, love?*

"No," said Eisl, his voice shaking. "No. No, I don't remember that. People don't—remember things from before they were born."

Oh, said the god after a moment, as if disappointed. *But... I loved you.*

Eisl wanted to cry with terror. "Why?"

You were trapped, and I was also trapped. She gave me bread and apples, she gave me meat and eggs and butter, she asked for all kinds of things. I looked up and I saw you; we spoke; I loved you. You wanted to be free. I want to be free too. You know what it's like, to be imprisoned. You knew even then —

"T-trapped? You're trapped?" Eisl had never heard anything like that, not in all the stories. Perhaps the god was lying to him. Perhaps it was trying to lure him out onto the bridge as so it could tip him off and kill him, as it sometimes had in the old days, decades ago, long before Eisl was born...

But he had been born. He'd been born because his mother had made a foolish bargain, and no matter how she tried to cheat, the thing in the ravine—spirit, god, ghost, who knew what it was—had not allowed harm to come to the infant...

Why? For what reason had the god remained so obsessed with him? How safe was a god's love? Was it even the same thing that humans understood love to be? Or was it greater than that, the sort of love that would overtake Eisl like a landslide and crush him under the weight and power of it?

Eisl was reminded powerfully of one of the very young children in the village—only four or five years old—who had found a mother cat and her newborn kittens in the barn, nestled in the hay. She had been so delighted with them that she had hugged each of the kittens so hard that they'd died.

Was that not comparable to him and the god? Was he not as powerless and helpless as a newborn kitten, in comparison to the god of the ravine?

Love, the god said, coaxing. *You'll take me with you, won't you?*

Eisl fled, scrambling away from the edge until he collapsed three-quarters of the way down the forest path and had to lie on the leaf mould and shake violently for a few minutes, wheezing for breath.

The world was not for him, then—would never be for him. He would remain in the village for all his days; he would never again approach the ravine.

E ISL RETURNED TO THE village and tried not to feel crushed with humiliation about it. He'd said goodbye to all of the villagers when he and Ylfing had been about to leave; doubtless they had heard about how he'd been sitting out by the bridge for days.

No one said anything to him, but there were looks—up-and-down looks at him, little huffs of contempt or disdain or amusement; pointed looks between two people, as if one of them was saying to the other, "Didn't I tell you he'd be back?"

But that was the way of the village. If a problem or an anomaly could be ignored, it would be.

Eisl couldn't bring himself to return immediately to the goatherding. Fortunately, after the first night sleeping in his own bed again, he woke up with a bad cold and a fever—his aunt, who had been glowingly pleased with his return, insisted that he stay in bed and rest. On any other day—any day before the day Ylfing had come, anyway—he would have protested. A little cold was no reason to shirk his duties, and no one else in the village was quite so good with the goats as he was. But today of all days, he wanted nothing more than to lie in bed and agree that he felt just dreadful, and be plied with soup and pine-and-honey tea, and then cry to himself when he'd been left alone in the room again.

The next day, he felt generally better physically, as well as guilty enough that he forced himself out of bed and began to pitch in with house chores, even while his aunt fussed over him and insisted one more day of rest would do him good.

He was sitting in a chair in front of the cabin door and shelling peas when Wren, one of the other young people of the village, a girl of about thirteen, ran up to him, red faced and panting. She had to lean on her knees for a moment and wheeze to catch her breath.

"What's wrong?" Eisl asked.

"Goats," she gasped. "Escaped and ran off. Nelo got most of them but he can't find the rest—asks if you can please come and help."

Eisl hurried to move the baskets of peas inside, calling back out to Wren, "Does he know which ones he's missing?" They all had different personalities, different habits...

"No?" Wren said, perplexed. "How can you tell them apart? They're all brown."

"Practice," Eisl said. A year or two of mostly staring at goats all day and you couldn't help but learn how to tell them apart.

He jogged up the mountain path to the grazing meadow, Wren trotting along beside him and making worried noises.

"Shouldn't we go faster?" she kept asking.

"We'll need our energy to catch the goats when we find them," he answered the first time, and then ignored her every subsequent time. There weren't many predators on the mountains, not this high up, and it was mostly rough terrain and steep slopes on the side of the ledge opposite the bridge and the ravine.

When they arrived at the meadow, Nelo was counting the goats with a frustrated expression; he turned to them as they ran up and cried out, "Eisl, I hate these things! Papa said it was easy, but they keep running off and I can't catch them! I had more earlier, I know I had more!"

Eisl cast his eye across the flock—he had the knack, his uncle had said, of not seeing the flock as a single whole which would have had to be counted to determine whether one was short of goats, as Nelo had been doing, but rather of seeing the flock as a group of individuals so that just by glancing across the flock he could tell *which* goats were missing. A much more useful skill.

His heart fell as he noticed which ones were absent. He didn't name them, because they were not pets and would be either slaughtered for the village or driven down to the market in the town—but nevertheless, he knew them as individuals.

There were three goats missing. One of them (call it Goat #1) was lively and curious, always trying to play with what Eisl assumed was the goat equivalent of a best friend—and that was Goat #2. Goat #2, additionally, did not have a particularly strong personality of its own, content to graze quietly and follow close behind one of the leaders of the flock wherever it led. The part that made Eisl cringe in uneasiness was that Goat #3 was one of these leaders, and *this* goat had an uncanny obsession with the ravine.

It was forever staring off in that direction, or trying to turn aside off the path to wander that way. If Eisl took his eyes off Goat #3 for a moment, it would trot right off, back down the path. Once, it had even made it as far as the forest, when Eisl had been occupied helping one of the other goats through a tricky birth.

He hadn't encountered the goats on the path up here, which meant... they were down on the ledge and probably had made it to the ravine by this point—Goat #3 stubbornly and intently making its way to the ravine, and Goat #2 following along brainlessly in its wake, and Goat #1 gamboling around them and trying to tease Goat #2 into responding.

Fuck.

"They're, um. They're down by the ravine," Eisl said, a cold knot of fear settling in his stomach. He almost opened his mouth to suggest that he could stay here and mind the rest of the goats while Wren and Nalo went below to fetch back the wandering trio....

But then he looked at them and saw *children,* even more helplessly kittenish than he was. Wren was thirteen; Nalo, her cousin, was about the same. No matter how terrified Eisl was of the ravine and the god trapped at the bottom of it, he *couldn't* send off children to do that work.

And he *was* better with the goats than anyone else in the village.

He groaned and rubbed his face. "Stay here. I'll bring them. Oh, and mind the one with the funny ear, it's about to start a fight with that other one."

He took a breath, turned back, kept his eyes down so he wouldn't catch a glimpse of the horizon, or the break in the trees where the ravine ran, or a wisp of mist rising from it.

He ran, hoping against hope that the goats had gotten distracted with something, that he'd find them nibbling contentedly on somebody's washing. He hoped while he stopped by the goat barn for a few lengths of rope. He hoped as he scanned his eyes around the village as he ran through.

He kept hoping all the way to the ravine, where he found Goat #1 munching with great interest on what must have been a particularly delicious clump of grass, because #2 and #3 were nowhere in sight.

Mouth dry, Eisl crept up to the goat and looped a length of rope around its neck.

The others are down here, whispered the god. Eisl nearly jumped out of his skin, his heart pounding and his hands shaking.

He realized a moment later that he'd gotten a rather strange emotional impression from that one sentence. An impression that had made his heart instinctively soften, made him look towards the ravine not out of concern but...

"Please don't hurt them," he whispered, though somehow he knew suddenly—as if deep down in some part of his soul, there was an awareness and a secret knowledge beginning to awaken—that the god in the ravine wouldn't hurt the goats.

At the same moment, the god whispered, *Hurry, please. I don't want them down here.*

Was the god *afraid* of the goats?

Surely not. He was a god. What call did a god have to be afraid of anything?

But the thought gave Eisl enough courage to tie off Goat #1 to one of the pine trees and creep close to the lip of the ravine and peer down.

Two goats, right at the bottom. Goat #3 drinking from the river. Goat #2 standing nearby, looking around like the empty-headed dolt it was and occasionally opening its mouth in what would have been a loud bleat of *Mehhh!* had it not been drowned out by the roar of the river.

The sheer drop knocked the breath out of Eisl's lungs. "How—how did they get down there?"

They climbed. Come upstream, there is a place.

Eisl knew then, vaguely, what spot the god must be talking about—he'd heard people talking about places where it was possible to climb down into the ravine, but in his terror of it, he had never explored the edges in any great detail. Or any detail.

He went along upstream and found, only a dozen yards further onwards, a place where a pile of huge boulders provided a very steep, uneven slope down. A *slope,* crucially. The boulders were big enough that he could drop from one to the other as he went down, and scramble back up with little more difficulty, though on the way back up he would have a pair of bothersome goats to deal with.

He sat on the edge and lowered himself the yard or so to the first stone. It had a few patches of moss and a clump of clearly goat-chewed grass, but although everything was damp with the constant rising moisture of the mists, the surface of the rocks was rough enough not to be slippery.

He stood, and reflected that he was, even now, technically *in the ravine.* His terror had melted into a numbness, as if the parts of his heart or his brain responsible for feeling the sensations of emotion had simply given up in protest. He could still feel the distant high-pitched drone of terror, like a ringing in his ears or the distant roar of the river when he was up in the grazing pasture with the goats, but that was all it was. A mosquito whine in the back of his mind, no more than a distraction as he made his way down the rocks and deeper into the ravine.

Halfway down, he glanced up and marveled distantly that he could barely even see the edges of the trees anymore. The trees had seemed as ever-present as the mountains and the ravine itself, but now it was as if he were descending into some mysterious other world where trees were nothing more than a rumor or a myth. Like he was descending into the afterlife, or the... Well, he supposed it *was* the realm of the gods in some sense.

The air got thicker and moister as he went down, dropping from boulder to boulder. The light got dimmer, too, though there was still plenty to see by—as dim as an overcast winter day, gloomy and subdued.

The god did not speak, which Eisl was grateful for. Whether or not the rocks were slippery, one word at the wrong time and Eisl might have startled and fallen.

He dropped off the last boulder and was astonished to find himself on the rocky, pebble-crusted riverbank.

Goat #2, not far distant, looked up at him and yelled, "Mehh!"

"Come here, you little twit," Eisl muttered, picking his way over the uneven ground.

Take them away now, said the god.

"I'm trying," Eisl said, reaching the two goats, who wandered amiably up to him and nosed at his hands in interest, lipping at the fabric of his tunic and trousers to see whether it was food. "There, yes, it's me, hello," he said to them, pulling the second length of rope from his belt and looping it around Goat #3's neck. "Come along now, you don't belong down here."

Certainly they don't, the god said with what amounted to a haughty sniff. *But then, nobody does. Take them away, make them leave.*

Eisl had no idea what possessed him to ask, considering that he was standing in this realm of a god, entirely at its—his—mercy, but he was distracted enough with coaxing the goats that his tongue moved without his say-so as he tugged Goat #3 along by its rope lead: "Why do they make you so uncomfortable?"

Their eyes. Unnatural. And I can't hide myself from them. In the old days, there were a few that were nearly wild, and they used to come down here all the time and stare at me.

And I can't get away from them when they do, the god concluded, this part spoken in a smaller voice than before—or giving the impression of a smaller, quieter voice, because everything within Eisl's head happened at roughly the same volume.

Eisl pulled Goat #3 up to the base of the rock pile before he bent and hauled it over his shoulders, binding its legs so that if it wriggled on the way up, it couldn't fall.

He mounted up the first boulder with only a bit more difficulty, and the god made an alarmed little noise. *Oh! Oh, you've left one! Don't leave this one behind! It's as bad as all the rest.*

"It's going to follow," Eisl said, heaving up onto the next rock. "It doesn't want to be separated from this one.

It'll follow. It got itself down, it can get itself back up."

Oh...

Eisl climbed, the exertion taking up his every spare thought as he maneuvered carefully up the steep slope. Gratifyingly, he did hear the other goat following along behind him, the clatter of its hooves on the rock, the occasional objecting cry of "Mehhh!"

He was winded when he reached the top, and as soon as he'd tied the goat to a tree so it couldn't go back down the second he took his eyes off it, he collapsed onto the ground and panted, coughing lightly as his lungs got working.

Yes, go on, shoo! said the god, as the last goat leapt nimbly up behind Eisl onto the solid ground at the edge of the forest. *Don't let them come back,* he added, sounding almost petulant. *I don't like them.*

"I'll do my best," Eisl said distractedly, nabbing the last goat and tying the other end of the rope around its neck—he was almost certain that it would follow brainlessly as it always did, but... better safe than sorry. He had no wish to go back down into the ravine again today. As strong as he was from a lifetime of living on the ledge and years of tending the goats, that climb had winded him.

He dragged the two goats back over to the third, untied it from the shrub, and got them to follow him towards the path that led back to the village.

Goodbye, the god whispered mournfully, just barely a wisp of a whisper in the back of Eisl's mind.

T HE THOUGHT OF IT stuck with him all the way back up to the goat field, and all the rest of the day as he shelled peas and split firewood for his aunt.

The god hadn't hurt him. Hadn't hurt the goats, even though he was frightened of them—or at least found them unpleasant enough to want nothing to do with them.

Going down into the ravine had been, in hindsight... exciting. It was a place he had never been before, full of mysteries and frightful things, but he'd done it.

He'd been so occupied with the goats and so eager to get out as soon as possible that it was only in remembering and reliving it afterward that he began to notice things about those brief moments. In his memory, the sides of the ravine seemed impossibly steep, impossibly tall; the gap between was narrow and cramped and restrictive, the noise of the water almost deafening, the mist clammy and cold, the strip of sky above a mere ribbon. What it must be like, to be trapped down there? Imprisoned, in a narrower cell than even the ledge and its grazing meadows and forests, unable to see the world laid out to the horizon, the broad sweep of sky bordered by the peaks of the mountains on either side and behind?

The next day, Eisl went back to the ravine, his heart still fluttering with habitual remembered fear in his chest. "Hello," he said tentatively.

The god didn't quite answer, but Eisl became aware of his attention, as if he'd looked up and was waiting expectantly for Eisl to say something more.

"I was wondering," Eisl said, his mouth dry. "I was wondering if I could ask you some questions."

If you like, I suppose.

"Where do you... come from?"

Here.

"The ledge?"

Yes.

Not a very helpful answer. "Why are you trapped?"

I don't know. I came down into the ravine one day for... something. I can't remember what it was. Something important. I came down for it, and when I found it, I couldn't leave. The others lowered food for me in baskets, or tossed it down, but it was no good. I built a hut out of rocks and branches, and they tossed down firewood for me, but I couldn't survive long. I froze, the first winter. I woke, and my body was there, but my soul had come loose. Like a child losing a tooth.

I lost myself, then, the god said, half-dreamy. *I don't remember anything for a long time. The others left, after they found I'd died. They had no reason to stay. I remember that.*

And the Great Ones were heading south; we used to follow them in those days.

"In...those days? How long ago was that? What Great Ones, what does that mean?"

The Great Ones. You know them. I'm sure you've seen them, love. Not so high up here in the mountain, they don't come up this far. But you must have seen them down on the plain, wandering in big herds.

But it wasn't a plain anymore, down below. It was farmland and forest. "I've never seen one."

The god sighed. *There were fewer the year I died than there had been the first year I learned to hunt. Perhaps they have all been killed... No matter, it is none of our concern. The Great Ones are like your goats, but a hundred times larger, and hairier, and each one a great... a great... an arm, hanging from its face. A nose, but also an arm. Like a snake, but it's for grabbing leaves and grasses to eat, or for drinking. And its horns were not on the top of its head, but on either side of its mouth. Great curving horns, smooth like polished wood, the color of bone, longer than you are tall.*

"Do you know how long ago that was?"

No. Long. LONG. The ravine was only a gully, then. Standing in the bottom, my I could have rested my chin on the edge.

Eisl looked at the expanse of the ravine, the dizzying depth of it, and felt nothing but a furiously buzzing incomprehension, like his mind was a jostled beehive.

I was lost for a time, the god said. *I could not begin to keep track of the years until the people came again, seeking for the stones in the mountain that—oh! I remember. I was looking for a stone. That's why I came down into the gully. There was a stone I was curious about. It was lying at the bottom of the stream.*

The fact that the god had been in the ravine since before people came to live on the ledge—since the days when the ravine's depth had been less than the height of a grown man—that was not the shocking part. Far more shocking was that he had once been alive. Had once been *human.*

It sent a wash of relief through Eisl's whole body—something in him relaxed and loosened, like the beginnings of snowmelt swelling the river's banks in spring. "You don't know what trapped you?"

The rock, I expect, the god said, now much more confidently. *It must have been that rock.*

"Do you know anything about the rock? Do you still have it?"

A beat of quiet. Eisl pictured the god looking around himself curiously. *No, I don't think I do. I think it was all washed away, a long time ago. The water washes rocks away if it has time.*

"But you're still trapped?"

Yes. The spirit of the rocks stay, even when their bodies are gone. The spirit goes into new rocks.

Eisl didn't know anything about spirits, and nothing about rocks beyond the ones that the miners chipped out in wagonloads from deep in the dark cracks of the earth.

He licked his lips, tasted the damp, the pine forest, the mist. There was a wisp of blue mist drifting along the bottom of the ravine. "But you asked me to take you with me. When I was trying to cross the bridge. How can you leave, if you're trapped?"

Mm, said the god, absently. *That other one told me.*

The other one. "The one I was trying to leave with?"

He came and spoke to me. He told me stories and helped bring me back to myself. A strange, eerie laugh that almost sounded like it echoed out of the ravine itself, rather than being whispered directly into Eisl's mind. *I was a little mad before that, I think. Even with you here, I was... I still am... lost. It feels like a dream—it's always felt like a dream. But ever since that one came and spoke to me, now I remember what dreams feel like.*

A gusty sigh, like winds through the ancient pines. *I shall lose myself again, in time. I shall lose count of the passage of days and the turn of the stars. The other one told me how he thought I might be freed.*

Eisl swallowed. "What did he say?"

It was ever so complicated, the god said with a petulant sniff. *He spoke nonsense words in some barbarian tongue— words I don't know, for no one speaks to me often. Your mother did, but no one else. He said... He said I was bound to the rocks on the riverbed. But I knew that. He said if someone took a rock with some of the right spirit in it, and carried it off, then I could cling to it and go too. He told me how it had happened once with some kind of flower. He said he couldn't take me, because he was looking for someone, and he didn't want to have to abandon me by the side of the road. But he said you might. He said I should ask.*

Eisl's stomach clenched in terror—but it was terror of crossing the bridge, not terror of the god.

How long had he been trapped here? How many hundreds of years had it taken for the water to cut the ravine this deep? Eisl pictured *centuries*, slowly watching the ribbon of sky above get smaller and smaller, watching the sides of the ravine get taller and steeper, watching the light grow dim.

"Can you tell which rocks have the right... spirit? The ones you could follow somewhere else?"

The god was silent for a moment. Then, slowly, he asked, *Are you offering, love?*

The whispering into the back of Eisl's mind meant he could feel the texture of emotion with much greater complexity than was possible to intuit in regular conversation. The words were almost teasing, almost flirtatious, but underlying that was a swelling surge of hope, like the river rising in the spring as the snows on the mountains began to melt away.

Hope. Simple, human hope. The same hope Eisl had felt when he'd thought of leaving with Ylfing and stepping out to see the wide world...

"I'm not making any promises," he said, his voice shaking a little. "I'm not promising to carry it forever. But." He swallowed, looked at the bridge, the path onwards through the forest, that *other* whisper in the back of his mind calling him towards adventure and a life bigger than what he had on the ledge. "But," he said. "I'll at least take a couple rocks somewhere else. And if we part, if I don't want to go onwards anymore, I'll leave them somewhere nice. A place you can see the whole sky, at least. A place that isn't so small and cramped."

Deal, said the god immediately. *Deal. A good bargain.*

Eisl's heart was pounding. He looked again at the bridge, at that last and greatest obstacle. Dry mouthed, he said, "And in return, you'll have to help me across."

Oh love, the god of the ravine said, the voice in Eisl's head brimming with sly fondness. *That won't be a challenge at all.*

ALSO BY ALEXANDRA ROWLAND

THE HISTORIES OF ARTHWEND

AND THE WIDE WORLD:

A Taste of Gold and Iron (forthcoming)

The Tales of the Chants:

A Conspiracy of Truths

A Choir of Lies

Over All the Earth

The Seven Gods Series:

Some by Virtue Fall

The Lights of Ystrac's Wood (forthcoming)

OTHER WORKS:

In The End

Finding Faeries

"In Our Own Image: Radical Empathy, Trickster Gods, and the Importance of Being Irritating"

About the Author

Alexandra Rowland is the author of *A Conspiracy Of Truths, A Choir of Lies, Some By Virtue Fall,* and *A Taste of Gold and Iron* (forthcoming Summer 2022 from Tor.Com Publishing), as well as a Hugo Award-nominated podcaster, all sternly supervised by their feline quality control manager. They hold a degree in world literature, mythology, and folklore from Truman State University.

Find them and more of their work at www.alexandrarowland.net, or on Patreon, Twitter, and Instagram as @_alexrowland.

Ingram Content Group UK Ltd.
Milton Keynes UK
UKHW011402050623
422897UK00004B/228

9 781957 461014